This book belongs to
_____

This book is dedicated to my children - Mikey, Kobe, and Jojo.

Copyright © 2024 Grow Grit Press LLC. All rights reserved. No part of this book may be reproduced in any form without permission in writing from the publisher. Please send bulk order requests to info@ninjalifehacks.tv

Paperback ISBN: 978-1-63731-992-5
Hardcover ISBN: 978-1-63731-994-9
eBook ISBN: 978-1-63731-993-2

Printed and bound in the USA.
NinjaLifeHacks.tv

Ninja Life Hacks®
by Mary Nhin

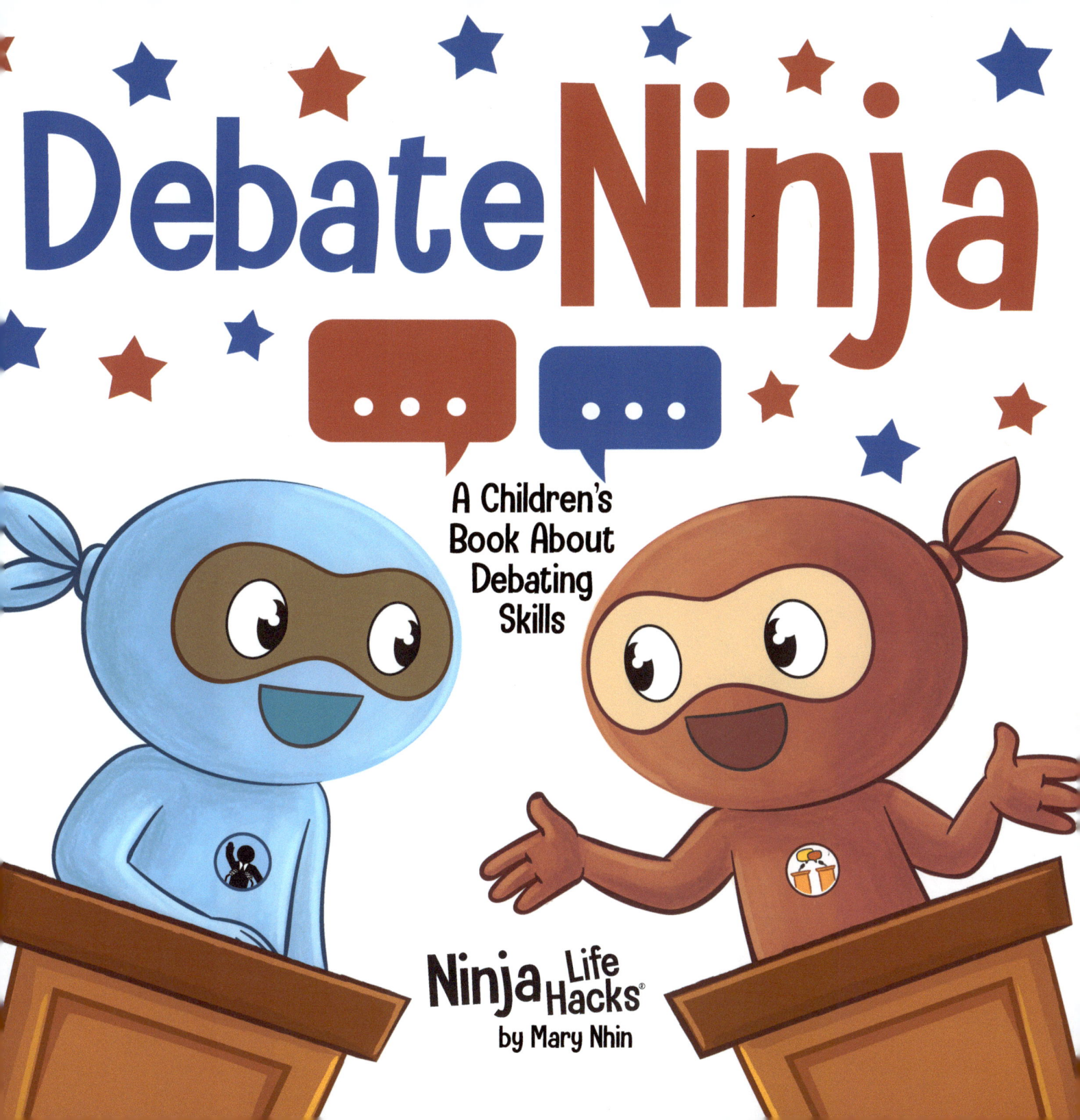

Then one day, President Ninja shared a life hack with me on how to handle debates using the S.P.E.A.K. technique.

Debate Ninja, it's okay to have different opinions, but it's important to debate respectfully. Try this:

 S: Speak Clearly

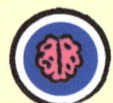 P: Prepare

 E: Ears to Hear

 A: Argue Respectfully

 K: Keep Calm

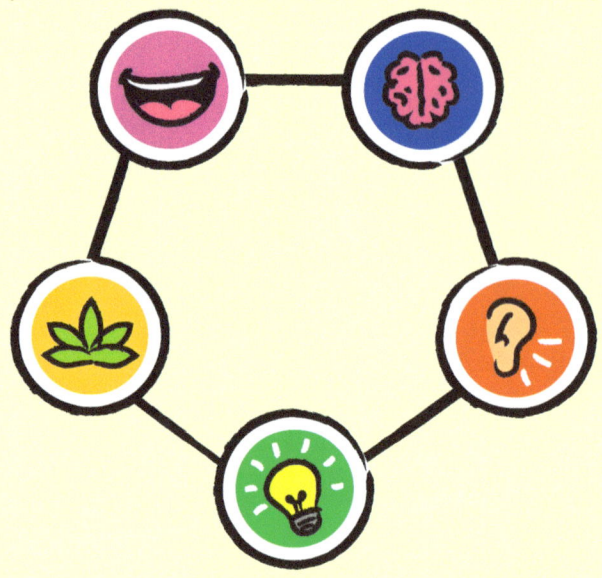

 S: Speak Clearly

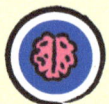 P: Prepare

 E: Ears to Hear

 A: Argue Respectfully

 K: Keep Calm

Remembering the S.P.E.A.K. strategy can help you become a great debater!

Check out the fun Debate Ninja lesson plans at ninjalifehacks.tv

I love to hear from my readers. Email me your feedback or thoughts on what my next story should be at info@ninjalifehacks.tv   Yours truly, Mary

 @marynhin   @GrowGrit   #NinjaLifeHacks

 Mary Nhin   Ninja Life Hacks

 Ninja Life Hacks

 @officialninjalifehacks

www.ingramcontent.com/pod-product-compliance
Lightning Source LLC
Chambersburg PA
CBHW042148200426
43209CB00066B/1822